Being Woke at Work

A workplace handbook of political correctness

Robert G. Cathcart

Contents

Introduction — 4

Workplace Inadequacy — 6

Physical Attraction — 13

Unproductiveness — 18

Physical Repulsion — 23

Expression of Sexuality — 32

Art of Articulation — 38

Ancient Antiquities — 45

Utter Unintelligence — 52

Antagonistic Attitudes — 70

Just so you're aware — 80

Introduction

As we navigate the current quagmire of political incorrectness, sexism, ageism, stupidism and other similar issues, we're gradually gaining ground on the road to acceptability. It's astonishing to believe that we used to get away with saying half of the things we've said in past jokes and attempts to conduct business or personal relationships.

This little booklet serves as a light-hearted memory bank of the best of the comments and sayings due to disappear from existence, as the Karens of the world continue to scour the internet, wiping it clean and eradicating all that was once considered humorous decades ago. I have tried my best to categorise these memories, but there may be some deviations from the plot, so bear with me on those uncategorisable must-includes. I scoured the net for weeks, painfully enduring at least thirty childish, unfunny phrases for each of the ones that I deemed worthy of inclusion. If the best part of your job is the fact that your chair swivels, you'll find plenty to smile about here. Just be prepared to hold your smile if you come across familiar material. It's not an attempt at originality; rather, it's a big collection of the best of the existing put-downs gathered together for posterity.

Workplace Inadequacy

Once deemed Tradesman-apprentice speak, foreman-labourer speak or even teacher-pupil speak. Terms like these were commonplace in workplace and classroom situations where frustrated bosses and teachers needed to vent at, well useless juniors of sorts. You know the scene – it exists more so than ever nowadays. The boss leaves an employee a task to do and comes back to find the job's an absolute shambles and no amount of money's worth has been got. Twenty years ago, the following were acceptable things to shout, nowadays its more than the boss's job is worth to open their mouth. Aimed at people who aren't very helpful to have around and can also be read as, "You're as helpful as…", here's the latest and best of the oldest, "you are useless" quotes…

Here's what **not** to say…

You're as much use as a one-armed taxi driver with crabs.

You're as much use as a cock flavoured lollipop.

You're as much use as a librarian with Tourette's.

You're as much use as a one-legged man in an arse-kicking contest.

You're as much use as a waterproof teabag.

You're as much use as a wooden frying pan.

You're as much use as a chocolate kettle.

You're as much use as an inflatable dartboard.

You're as much use as a glass hammer.

You're as much use as an accordion player on a deer hunt.

You're as much use as a trapdoor on a lifeboat.

You're as much use as a hide-and-seek player with Tourette's.

You're as much use as a chocolate teapot.

You're as much use as an ashtray on a motorbike.

You're as much use as a handbrake on a canoe.

You're as much use as an ejector seat in a helicopter.

You're as much use as a Shortbread cricket bat.

You're as much use as a chocolate fireguard.

You're as much use as a carpet fitter's ladder.

You're as much use as a knitted condom.

You're as much use as a woodpecker with rubber lips.

You're as much use as the g in lasagne.

You're as much use as the ay in okay.

You're as much use as balls on a dildo.

You're as much use as a left-handed football bat.

You're as much use as <u>a</u> chopstick.

You're as much use as a soup sandwich.

You're as much use as tastebuds in your bum.

You're as much use as the vowels in queue.

You're as much use as a porcupine in a balloon factory.

You're as much use as a lava lamp.

You're as much use as a rubber cheese grater.

You're as much use as a solar powered torch.

You're as much use as an indoor sundial.

You're as much use as girls' jeans pockets.

You're as much use as a hand towel on a life raft.

You're as much use as a monkey with a machine gun.

You're as much use as a Californian umbrella.

You're as much use as a chocolate teaspoon.

You're as much use as pork pies at a Jewish wedding.

You're as much use as a grave robber in a crematorium.

You're as much use as mudguards on a tortoise.

You're as much use as <u>a</u> walkie-talkie.

You're as much use as a basket of hot soup with a polystyrene fork.

You're as much use as a velociraptor at a hugging contest.

You're as much use as nipples on a suit of armour.

You are as much use as a one-armed trapeze artist with an itchy arse.

You're as useless as a screen door on a submarine.

You are as much use as Captain Hook in an emergency Caesarean section.

You're as much use as the sink on the space station.

You're as much use as an electric sundial.

You're as much use as a sponge helmet.

You're as much use as a library for a Tourette's meeting.

You're as much use as a fish-net condom.

Physical Attraction

Come-ons and chat-up lines from the nineties – not now considered useable. Just to get you up to speed (if you happen to be Rip Van Winkle) – There was a decade when these sayings would earn you a partner. It was followed by a decade where they'd get you laughed at, subsequently followed by a decade where saying any of this out loud would result in a red handprint on your cheek. We're now in a decade where these sayings could earn you a prison sentence. Perhaps you should just hold on to them and see what the next decade brings. In the meantime however …

Here's what **not** to say...

You make me wetter than Stevie Wonder's toilet seat.

I'd fuck your shadow on a gravel path.

Well here I am! What are your other two wishes.

I wish I was cross-eyed so I could see you twice.

My name is Henri but you can call me tonight.

I'm not into watching sunsets, but I'd love to see you go down.

It's girls like you that cause global warming.

If you were fruit you'd be a fineapple.

I may not go down in history, but I will go down on you.

Are you into fitness? How about you fitness dick in your mouth?

I have a chocolate penis which ejaculates money.

I don't like being told what to do unless I'm naked.

You're so pretty my trousers are falling for you.

You know, if I were you, I'd have sex with me.

I'm so jealous of your heart…
Why ?
It's pounding away inside you and I'm not.

Are you a tortilla? Because I want to flip you over and eat you out.

I'd love to kiss those beautiful, luscious lips. And the ones on your face.

Are you a middle eastern dictator? Cause there's a political uprising in my pants.

Are you a haunted house? Because I'm going to scream when I'm in you.

Did you make Santa's naughty list this year? Do you want to?

Do you have room for an extra tongue in your mouth? or anywhere?

Are you a supermarket sample? Because I want to taste you again and again without any sense of shame.

Excuse me, but does my tongue taste funny to you?

Are you a sea lion? Because I can see you lion in my bed tonight.

As long as I have a face, you'll have a place to sit.

I'm like a Rubik's Cube; The more you play with me, the harder I get.

My dick died; Do you mind if I bury it in your ass?

Do you like whales? Because we can go hump back at my place.

What's the difference between a Ferrari and an erection? I don't have a Ferrari.

I'm trying to stop using sexual innuendos but you're making it hard.

I'm not a weatherman, but you can expect a few more inches tonight.

If I flip a coin, what are my chances of getting head?

Let's play house. You can be the door then I can slam you all I want.

If you were a door I'd slam you all night.

I'm not a dentist, but I'd give you a filling.

Are you an archaeologist? Because I've got a large bone for you to examine.

Your body is 70 percent water… and I'm thirsty.

That's a nice shirt. Can I try it on after we have sex?

I think you're suffering from a lack of vitamin me.

If you're feeling down, I can feel you up.

What is a nice person like you doing in a dirty mind like mine?

I think I could fall madly in bed with you.

Are you my homework? Because I should be doing you.

Fuck me if I'm wrong, but dinosaurs still exist right?

Are you a drill sergeant? Because you have my dick standing at attention.

Would you like to go halves on a baby?

You need a hug, in your vagina, with a penis.

Unproductiveness

Every workplace has at least one lazy colleague who'd be happy to waste everybody's time and get nothing done. They're like wind-up soldiers who seem to run out of oomph the instant the boss looks away. If you're the kind of person who goes above and beyond you'd probably end up having to do extra work to compensate for these individuals. Watching them chat and wondering how they get away with it all day boils your piss. You fantasise about sneaking up and blasting a train horn behind them and screaming obscenities in their face but you know you can't. You've signed a contract and must stick to a script…

Here's what **not** to say...

Well if you don't do any work you won't make any mistakes.

Don't mistake my efficiency as meaning that I want to have your job too.

If there was an award for laziness you would probably send someone to go pick it up for you.

Oh, you can do my job? Funny, I haven't seen you do yours just yet.

Pretending to look busy on a Friday is the hardest work you do all week.

I'm not asking you for a favour… I'm telling you to do your job.

Sorry, I wasn't aware that "lazy f*ck" is part of your job description. I will be more considerate next time I ask for something.

Oh, that task isn't in your job description? Well dealing with your bullshit isn't in mine.

Your out-of-office reply is responding to more emails than you ever do.

Why don't you try something a little more relaxing, like a coma?

Have you got a snooze button on your smoke alarm?

Have a seat, standing there watching everyone else work all day must be exhausting.

I don't think of you as a co-worker because you never do any work.

Have you got emotional constipation cos you haven't given a shit for days?

If there was work in your bed you'd lie on the floor.

I can explain it to you but I can't understand it for you.

You're so lazy you'd marry a pregnant woman.

If I wanted to pick up lazy people's shit I'd have worked on a farm.

What's with the selective participation ?

You'd rather enter a coma than a gym.

You're so lazy you get excited about cancelling plans.

You're like a motion sensor the way you start working when I'm passing.

If there was an award for laziness you'd send someone to pick it up for you.

Oh you identify as a lazy person? Well I identify as the CEO, get the fuck off my premises.

Physical Repulsion

Whether it's their face or the shape they are in, there are countless reasons for this and the total number of mentionable ones is zero. Here's some of the more common reasons for the lack of chemistry.

Your face/body shape is inadequate.

As much as it makes you wonder if some people burn more calories dragging that ass in from the carpark as you burn working a ten-hour shift, it isn't for you to decide which of you was created in God's image. If they consider the best form of exercise to be the diddly squat then that's their prerogative.

So… Even if you think you could easily escape wearing concrete boots.

Here's what **not** to say…

You couldn't get laid if you were an egg.

You look like a 'before' picture.

You're so fat you couldn't jump to a conclusion.

I bet your reflection walks away.

You haven't been inside a woman since you visited the Statue of Liberty.

Do you sometimes feel so sick of the world that you can't finish your second apple pie?

If you had a pound for every guy who didn't find you attractive, they'd find you attractive.

Have you considered suing your parents.

Don't let that extra chromosome get you down.

You look like I need a drink.

You look like something I'd doodle with my left hand.

I'm sorry for the cruel, horrible, and true things I said.

You're so ugly your portraits hang themselves.

Laughter is the best medicine. Sell your face to the chemist.

Don't put your head out the window; You'll get arrested for mooning.

You have a face only a mother could love.

You have less class than a school in the summer.

Behind every fat person there's someone beautiful. No seriously, you're in the way.

I never forget a person's face, but I'll be happy to make an exception in your situation.

It's not beauty sleep you need, its hibernation.

You can be whatever you want to be, except attractive.

If you were the light at the end of the tunnel, I'd turn back around.

I've met individuals like you but I had to pay for entry.

Beauty is skin deep; ugliness goes right to the bone.

You're so fat you could sell shade.

I've tried to get on your good side but its two bus journeys away.

Do bears hide their food when you go camping?

Were you poured into your clothes and you forgot to say "when"?

Is it gardening season? Since you planted your arse in the chair it's grown considerably.

Don't worry about me. Worry about your eyebrows.

People say that laughter is the best medicine… your face must be curing the world.

Life is short. Smile while you still have teeth.

I've seen better dressed wounds than you.

I see you were so impressed with your first chin that you added two more.

Do you open the post with that nose?

Do you have a pen? Well get back in it.

Nice teeth, brown is my favourite colour.

Your mother should've thrown you away and kept the stork.

You're a parasite for sore eyes.

You're ugly enough to make an onion cry.

Did your mum tie a pork chop round your neck so that the dog would play with you?

When you look in the mirror does your reflection duck?

Beauty is only skin deep; Ugly goes right to the bone.

Is that haircut to distract us from your face?

Have you ladies left Cinderella at home?

You have to love nature
even though it screwed you over.

You've a face like chewed toffee.

They say beauty's on the inside; You better hope that's true.

That triple chin is shaping up lovely.

You still love nature after what it did to you?

Did you apply that make-up with a shotgun?

If my dog looked like you I'd paint a face on his arse and teach him to walk backwards.

I just took a photo of you working but you're so fat it's still printing.

You're in great shape - shame the shape is round.

You've got double chins all the way down to your stomach.

Not only have you kept your lovely figure, **you've added so much to it.**

Don't lie on the beach. Greenpeace will push you back in the water.

You have more chins than a Hong Kong phone book.

You look like something I drew with my left hand.

You're sweating more than a blind lesbian in a fish market.

It must be great to wake up on both sides of the bed.

Are all those your chins or are you looking at me over a pile of pancakes?

Your body is a temple, albeit a temple of doom.

Hey, you have something on your chin…no, the third one down.

You're so fat I swerved to avoid you and ran out of petrol.

You're so fat you keep your purse under your folds.

I'd give you a bad look but you have one.

Respect your partner's stupid choices; You're one of them.

Your mother should've swallowed you.

You have a face that would scare a toilet.

Expression of sexuality

Reserving judgement is the way of the day. Your opinion, as expert as you believe it to be, must remain your own. Quote the company dress code if you will but don't attempt to estimate your colleagues' sexual experience, assume their attempts to lure a mate, assume the gender of that mate based on your colleagues' make-up, attire, conversation style or non-verbal cues.

Trying to be the modern-thinking person in a workplace full of dinosaurs can be just as confusing as being the dinosaur in a workplace full of modern-thinking twenty-somethings. There are still people out there who cannot adjust to the vision of free expressionism and feel threatened enough to create a snigger, even if just to see who's still on team snigger. All of the following could result in security being called to escort your big old dinosaur ass from your workplace premises.

Here's what **not** to say...

Excuse me but you have a bit of face on your make-up.

You look beautiful today, is that a new Instagram filter you're wearing?

You've a little bit of face on your make-up.

You're not quite as straight as the pole your mother dances on.

You're as camp as Christmas.

You're as camp as a row of tents.

You're as camp as glitter embossed tits.

You have less class than a school in the summer.

Maybe if you ate some of that makeup you could be pretty on the inside.

Nice perfume. Must you marinate in it?

Save your breath. You'll need it to blow up your girlfriend.

Nice tan, orange is my favourite colour.

They used to be called jumpolines until your wife jumped on one.

Your only flair is in your nostrils.

If you ever become a mother, can I have one of the puppies.

You've had more clap than an auditorium.

I bet you take crabs to the beach.

You're like the first slice of bread; everyone touches you yet nobody wants you.

I'd give you a dirty look, but you already have one.

I'd kick you in the vagina but I'm afraid I'd lose my shoe.

You've been rodgered more times than a policeman's walkie talkie.

Sex with you would be like doing push-ups over an open manhole.

Learn to take a joke as easily as you take a dick.

All that makeup won't make you look any less stupid.

You've stroked more wood than a furniture polisher.

You give away more pussy than the animal shelter.

If your vagina had a password, it'd be "1234".

I don't see any penises in the general vicinity... So I'm wondering why you keep opening your mouth.

You've seen more Japs' eyes than a Tokyo optician.

I'm not saying that you're a slut, but I see that your favourite shade of lipstick is penis.

Your makeup looks like something I drew with my left hand.

Your legs spread faster than Ebola.

You're not popular, your vagina is.

If dicks had wings, your mouth would be an airport.

What've you ever done? Besides everyone?

There's a person for everybody out there. It's a psychologist for you.

When you're doing your make-up tomorrow just remember this isn't a circus.

Not all gay people are happy, camp, and fun. Some are lesbians.

Art of Articulation

Every workplace has at least one person that we all struggle to understand. You know the situation too well… They speak, you say "pardon?" they repeat themselves with no attempt to be clearer. You say "what?" they say it louder but still don't bother to move their mouth. You resort to non-verbal clues such as laughter, and so you laugh along without a clue in hell what you're both laughing at. For all you know, they may have had a lazy tonsil since birth or something, still, they're not as bad as the people who can speak clearly but can't round off the conversation. I've been told that there are better ways to express the fact that someone hasn't got you riveted so…

Here's what **not** to say...

Ok try again but this time use your big boy words.

You're as confusing as fathers' day in the ghetto.

If you were a sports event you'd be The Mumble in the Jumble.

You should come with subtitles.

I just checked my calendar and I won't give a fuck next Tuesday either.

I may love to shop but I'd never buy your bull.

One day you'll choke on the crap you talk.

Check the time, it's time for you to shut up already!

I clapped because it's over, not because I enjoyed it.

I apologise if I made a noise with my eye roll.

Look! there goes the last fuck I gave.

Oh no! I left my sympathy for you lying next to a pile of I couldn't give two fucks at home.

Please keep speaking. I always yawn when I'm interested.

Good story, but in what chapter do you shut up?

I'm sorry, I didn't hear you over the sound of how much I don't care.

Your silence has a wonderful sound.

It's not necessary to say it again. I ignored you quite well the first time.

If bullshit was a music genre you'd be an orchestra.

Isn't your arse jealous of the shit that comes out your mouth?

If you were an insect you'd be a Mumble Bee.

If you'd gone up the hill with Jack, you'd have come mumbling down.

Silence is golden. Duct tape is silver.

Cancel my subscription because I don't need your issues.

Shut your mouth when you're talking to me.

You play the victim. I'll play the disinterested bystander.

My favourite thing to listen to is you not talking.

I bet your favourite pudding is rhubarb mumble and custard.

We all know someone who speaks fluent crap.

How many licks until I get to the interesting part of this conversation?

Here's a nice cup of I don't give a shit, You're welcome.

Do you mind if I hum while you talk?

Is your favourite movie George of the Jumble?

You definitely know which side your bread is muttered on.

Sorry, I'm not good at acting like I'm interested.

I think the fuck I gave went that way.

Ancient Antiquities

You know the bloke that was in the building the day your company bought it? He did his bit back in the day and now it would be unfair to open the door and let him wander off, so the company finds him some relic-related tasks. Knowing just how long he has till retirement is above your pay scale and asking him might give him the impression you are pushing him out the door. You'll know him when you see him and when you see him…

Here's what **not** to say...

I'm not saying you're old but if you were milk I'd sniff you.

I bet your candles cost more than your cake.

You'd make a stale raisin look smooth.

Do you burp dust?

I bet you remember when the Dead Sea was just ill.

Relax, the more birthdays you have, the longer you'll live.

Was there history when you were at school?

Do you oil your joints?

You still cut the mustard; You just need help opening the jar.

Being your age isn't so bad when you consider the alternative.

I bet you remember when Burger King was a prince.

Were you the lollipop man when Moses parted the Red Sea?

Congratulations on another year of not dying.

Was your National Insurance number 1?

Was Moses in your class photograph?

I bet your birthday parties are a fire hazard.

You have more wrinkles than an elephant's scrotum.

I bet you've seen honey expire.

Did Jurassic Park bring back memories?

Did archaeologists find ancient pottery in your vagina?

Don't let your age get you down; You'll struggle to get back up.

Is your memory in black and white?

Did you know Burger King while he was still a prince?

I bet your birthday cake looks like a forest-fire.

You're so old, you fart dust.

Has your birth-certificate expired?

The '80s called; They want their haircut back.

If you were whisky you'd be really expensive.

Did you know Gandalf before he had a beard?

One more wrinkle and you'd pass for a prune.

I hear that you're moving from the retirement home to the museum.

I bet you remember when the Grand Canyon was a ditch.

You're so old, the back of your head looks like a raisin.

You co-wrote the Ten Commandments, didn't you?

You're so old, you have an autographed bible.

You're so old, you knew Cap'n Crunch while he was still a private.

You're so old, you still remember the Spanish Flu.

You're so old you were probably a waitress at the Last Supper.

When you were a kid were rainbows in black and white?

I bet you know which testament is most accurate.

You're so old if you went to an antique store they wouldn't let you leave.

You look like my scrotum sack.

You're so old you shit fossils,

Have you got hieroglyphics on you driver's license?

Did you sit next to Ben Franklin in kindergarten.

Was the key on Ben Franklin's kite for your apartment?

Is your memory in black and white?

Did you drive a chariot to high school?

I think you baby-sat for Jesus.

You're so old you dated John the Baptist.

Did you grow up near the Flintstones?

You're so old you planted the apple tree in The Garden of Eden!

You're so old God signed your yearbook.

I bet you remember how they built the Pyramids of Giza.

You're so old you helped name the planets.

What was the birth of Jesus like?

When Moses parted the red sea were you on the other side fishing?

Was your first job shovelling shit on Noah's Ark?

You're so old you got to see passion of the Christ live!

You babysat Adam and Eve; Didn't you?

Did you sit next to Jesus in school?

Utter Unintelligence

Sometimes it's difficult to establish whether your co-workers are being stupid, being lazy, or being smart-lazy (secretly leading you to believe that they're stupid whilst outsmarting you into doing what the company is paying them to do). In most cases, it's the former. No matter how frustrated you feel, just remember not to resort to the infinite bank of metaphors for stupidity. Here's the better ones…

Here's what **not** to say…

The wheel's spinning but the hamster's dead.

It's ok if you disagree with me. I can't force you to be right.

You're not the sharpest knife in the drawer, are you?

You're a few clowns short of a circus.

If you had another brain it would be lonely.

It's because of people like you that shampoo bottles have instructions.

Who ties your shoes in the morning?

You're slower than moon tig.

Why is it okay for you to be a moron but inappropriate for me to call you out on it?

You're slower than a quadriplegic in a sack-race.

You should ask for a refund on that empty head.

Listen… don't home-school your kids.

You're as slow as molasses in January.

You're as quick as a herd of snails.

How long does it take you to watch 60 minutes?

You're as slow as a week in jail.

Don't think about it too hard. You'll sprain that brain.

I keep thinking you can't get any dumber and you keep proving me wrong.

You're slower than dial-up.

You're about a quick as an asthmatic snail.

You're slower than stop.

You're about as quick as the seven-year itch.

You must be robbing a village somewhere of their idiot.

You're slower than erosion.

You're slower than a one-fingered typist.

You have your whole life to be a moron. Let's skip today.

You're as quick as a stalactite.

You're proof evolution can go backwards.

You are what happens when pregnant women drink.

I'd insult you, but then I'd have to clarify it.

Don't feel bad. A lot of people have no talent.

Watching you attempt to use all of your vocabulary in a single statement is sort of funny.

I'd offend you, but I'm worried you'd miss it.

Humanity sprang from apes but I don't think you sprang far enough.

Do you have to work hard to be this stupid, **or is it just who you are?**

A thought crossed your mind?
That must've been a long, lonely trip.

You're as helpful as the g in lasagne.

It's impossible to underestimate you.

You're as sharp as a sack of soup.

You have miles to go before you reach mediocre.

I'm just glad that you're stringing words into sentences now.

Don't let your mind wander. It's too little to be out on its own.

You have delusions of adequacy.

Looks like the fuckup fairy has visited your thinking again.

I'd liked to have fucked your brains out but it appears that someone beat me to it.

The smartest thing ever to come out of your mouth was a penis.

You suck. You should fix that.

Sarcasm is the body's natural defence against stupidity.

I'm sorry I hurt your feelings when I called you stupid.

You'd be out of your depth in a baby bath.

You're not the crunchiest crisp in the bag.

If you don't want a sarcastic answer, then don't ask a stupid question.

You're a few bales short of a wagon load.

I don't understand what you're saying. I'm not fluent in Moron.

They say ignorance is bliss but I find yours rather disturbing.

My tolerance for idiots is extremely low today. I used to have some immunity built up, but obviously there is a new strain out there.

Your driveway doesn't quite reach the road.

You're not the quickest bunny in the forest.

You are to this job what Dr. Pepper is to medicine.

You are to this job what vomit is to foreplay.

You are to this job what acne is to self-confidence.

The lights have turned green but you haven't found the biting point.

The logs are burning but the chimney's clogged.

You're so dumb you'd get fired from a blowjob.

The wind's blowing but the washing's not drying.

You are to this job what a wasp is to a picnic.

You are to this job what Father Ted is to Catholicism.

You are to this job what lard is to dieting.

You are to this job what Officer Dibble is to law enforcement.

Are you the first in your family born without a tail ?

You're not yourself today; I noticed the improvement.

If you had a brain you'd be on the floor playing with it.

You're the reason the gene pool needs a lifeguard.

I'm glad to see you're not letting education get in the way of your ignorance.

I would prefer a battle of wits, but you appear unarmed.

I like the way you try.

If genius skips a generation, your children will be brilliant.

If you were an inanimate object, you'd be a participation trophy.

You have an entire lifetime to be an idiot.

Take today off.

Isn't it dangerous to use your whole vocabulary in one sentence?

If I had a pound for every time you said something smart, I'd be skint.

In the land of the witless, you would be king.

You're just spare parts; Aren't you bud?

Your train of thought is a replacement bus service.

If your brains were dynamite there wouldn't be enough to blow your hat off.

I've forgotten more than you ever knew.

Keep rolling your eyes, you might spot a brain back there.

The porch light is on but nobody's home.

You have a room temperature IQ.

What's on your mind? If you'll allow the overstatement.

You couldn't pour water out of a boot if the instructions were on the heel.

You must've had a brolly the day it rained brains.

Your antennae don't pick up all the channels, do they?

Your skylight leaks a little.

Were you an experiment in artificial stupidity?

I have neither the time nor the crayons to explain this to you.

You're as bright as a blackout.

The barriers are down, the lights are flashing but the train isn't coming.

Some drank from the fountain of knowledge but you just gargled.

You're so dense, light bends around you.

You're a prime candidate for natural deselection.

You're a couple of singers short of a barber shop quartet.

You have a photographic memory but the lens cap is still on.

You're as bright as Alaska in December.

When one door closes, another one opens. Or you can open the closed door. That's how doors work.

If you had brains you'd be dangerous.

Everything happens for a reason and sometimes you're the reason.

You're rolling like a flat tyre this morning.

You're as quick as a turtle running in peanut butter.

If bullshit could float you'd be an admiral in the navy.

I apologise if my common sense upset you.

Please don't use your entire vocabulary in the same sentence.

It's nice to see your ignorance isn't interfering with your education.

You're quite good at things till you have to do them.

Don't you have an empty feeling? In your skull?

You're a biscuit short of a packet.

I think your road to success is under construction.

If everything seems to be going well you must have overlooked something.

It's all fun and games until you don't pick up on my sarcasm.

Don't be so humble – you are not that great.

You're all foam and no beer.

Have no fear of perfection – you'll never reach it.

Zombies eat brains. You're quite safe.

You're a few sandwiches short of a picnic.

Did you sneak into the gene pool when the lifeguard wasn't looking?

The company cherishes their original misconception of you.

I'm allergic to stupidity; I break out in sarcasm.

I'd agree with you but then we'd both be wrong.

I could eat alphabetti spaghetti and shit a smarter statement than that.

The only time you shouldn't give 100% is when you're giving blood.

Everyone has the right to be stupid but you're abusing the privilege.

I'm sorry. Did the middle of my sentence interrupt the beginning of yours?

I'm not saying you're stupid but you have bad luck when it comes to thinking.

Your brain is a wonderful organ; it starts working the moment you open your eyes and doesn't stop until you get here.

Everything happens for a reason but sometimes the reason is because you're stupid and you make bad decisions.

People say nothing is impossible but you manage to do it every day.

You haven't failed. You've found twenty ways that don't work.

Studies have shown that intelligent people swear more than you stupid motherfucker.

Oh you hate your job. Why didn't you say so? There's a support group for that. It's called everybody, and they meet at the bar.

It's better to shut up and give the impression you're stupid than to say something and eradicate all doubt.

Honey, you're not pretty enough to be that stupid.

You're so stupid you make me squint.

I'm just thrilled you're putting words together now.

Make-up doesn't fix stupidity.

You didn't fall out of the stupid tree. You've been dragged through the forest of dumbass.

You're not the dumbest person in the world but you better hope he doesn't die.

If you continue speaking, I'll presume you badly require a dictionary.

Don't attempt to think too much. Your stupidity might injure your brain.

Antagonistic Attitudes

Personalities clash. It's a fact of life. Everyone is different and nobody comes to work to be liked. The measure of a professional colleague is one who can effectively communicate with bell ends without demonstrating any hint of their thoughts. As much as you'd like to on an hour-by-hour basis…

Here's what **not** to say...

Sometimes I need what only you can provide: Your absence.

If my opinions annoy you, you gotta hear the ones I keep to myself.

I'll never forget how we first met. But I'll keep attempting.

Would you like some cheese with that whine?

Oh sweetheart – I've got a fake laugh with your name written all over it."

Off is the general direction I'd like you to fuck.

I'd like to kill you with kindness, but all I have is a hammer.

Go lay in the backyard if you're going to behave like a turd.

I want to help you out. Which direction did you come from?

I bet your mother calls you a son of a bitch.

You'll never be half the man your mother is.

I apologize if my forced apology sounded fake; I'll work to improve it the next time.

Didn't I tell you? Well it must be none of your business.

May both sides of your pillow be uncomfortably warm.

I'm sorry I never texted you back. My dog ate the message.

You should really come with a warning label.

I will ignore you so hard you will start doubting your existence.

You see that door? I want you on the other side of it.

I am returning your nose. I found it in my business.

Who ate your bowl of sunshine this morning, thundercloud?

I'm sure your parents shift the topic when their friends ask about you.

I wouldn't piss on you if you were on fire.

You'd give an aspirin a sore head.

If I throw a stick, will you leave?

If I wanted to hear from an asshole I'd fart.

Keep still. I'm trying to picture you with a personality.

You are being described, not criticised.

Do you recall when I requested your opinion? neither do I.

I'm sorry; you mistook me for a person who cares.

Life is great, you better get one.

Can I ignore you later? I have a lot on right now.

I apologize for doing anything that made you believe I care about how you feel.

You give my middle finger a hard on.

Never mistake my silence for weakness.
Nobody plans a murder out loud.

People think I go out of my way to piss them off.
Trust me, it's not out of my way at all.

Sorry... to have met you.

Yeah, I'm a pacifist. I'm about to pass a fist across your face.

Underestimate me. That will be fun.

People need to start appreciating the effort I put in to not be a serial killer.

You were my cup of tea, but I drink champagne now.

Oops! Did I just roll my eyes out loud?

I'm sorry, I don't take orders. I barely take suggestions.

I'll see you in my dreams if I eat enough cheese.

I'll give you a going away present but you'll have to do your part first.

I'd like to see things from your perspective but I doubt there's room up your arse for both our heads.

I wish I'd more hands to show you more middle fingers.

I just heard about your illness. I hope it's nothing trivial.

Dealing with you is like nailing jelly to the wall.

You are a waste of oxygen.

I'd like to help you out; Which way did you come in?

You are the human version of a sore head.

I'd like you to go to hell but I work there and I don't want you showing up.

Roses are red, shit is brown, shut the fuck up and sit down.

I don't exactly hate you, but if you were on fire and I had water, I'd drink it.

I like long walks, especially when they are taken by you.

If you find it hard to laugh at yourself, I would be happy to do it for you.

Twinkle Twinkle little snitch, mind your business nosey bitch.

I was today years old when I realized I didn't like you.

Someday you'll go far. And I really hope you stay there.

Bye. Hope to see you never.

I'd rather treat my baby's diaper rash than have lunch with you.

Somewhere out there is a tree tirelessly producing oxygen for you. You owe it an apology.

That sounds like a you problem.

Remember that time you were saying that thing I didn't care about? Yeah, that is now.

Your secret's safe with me. I wasn't listening.

Don't be ashamed; That's your parents' job.

You have so many gaps in your teeth it looks like your tongue is in jail.

Don't worry about me. Worry about your eyebrows.

When you were born the doctor held you up and slapped your mum.

People like you are the reason God doesn't talk to us anymore.

You're a conversation starter.

Not when you are around, but once you leave.

First off: Brush your teeth.

You should carry a plant around with you to replace the oxygen you waste.

I'm not saying I hate you, what I'm saying is that you are literally the Monday of my life.

If you find me offensive. Then I suggest you quit finding me.

I'm sorry while you were talking I was trying to figure where the hell you got the idea I cared.

I don't have the energy to pretend to like you today.

If you're waiting for me to give a crap, you better pack a lunch. It's going to be a while.

Sorry for being late. I got caught up enjoying my last few minutes of not being here.

You're everything I want in someone I don't want anymore.

Sometimes I meet people and feel bad for their dog.

Pick my lowest priority and place yourself under it.

You need a high five, in the face, with a chair.

Just so that you're aware

(the serious side)

Inappropriate comments in the workplace can refer to the oral or written remark that makes a person feel awkward or hurt. While the criteria on what is appropriate for the organisation can differ depending on your workplace culture, there are always some offensive comments that people think inappropriate.

Even when individuals in an organisation can discuss sensitive matters and offer positive criticism to others, humiliating and taunting others or making intolerant comments is not acceptable workplace conduct. In addition, it is further crucial to have a tolerant environment and avoid making stereotypes about groups based on sexuality, gender, political affiliation, religion, or race.

An important aspect of working in a collaborative workplace is communicating with others and adding to a productive and positive environment. However, sometimes, people make comments during workplace discussions that are not appropriate for professional places for numerous reasons.

Understanding how to recognise and manage inappropriate comments can assist you in ensuring that you support a welcoming and safe working environment for all of your colleagues and customers. Furthermore, making racist or negative remarks also constitutes inappropriate comments. Here are some examples of inappropriate comments that you can overhear in a workplace.

Making detrimental remarks about an employee's personal religious views or attempting to convert them to a specific religious ideology, Using racist phrases, slang, or nicknames, Making comments about a person's skin tone or other ethnic attributes, Making lewd regards to a person's physical or mental disability

Sharing indecent photos, emails, videos, letters, or notes, Offensively speaking about averse ethnic, racial, or spiritual stereotypes, Making demeaning age-related comments

Transmitting sexually indecent pictures or videos, such as sensual gifs or pornography, with co-workers.

Sending figurative notes, letters, or emails, Displaying unsuitable sexual pictures or signs in the workplace, Telling offensive jokes, or sharing sexual stories, Improper touching, including patting, pinching, rubbing, or deliberately brushing up against someone, Gazing in a sexually lewd or abusive manner, or whistling.

It is important to address inappropriate comments in the organisation to ensure every employee feels safe and comfortable communicating as a team.

When a person makes a harsh or prejudiced statement directly to you or overhears a discussion in the organisation, you might become furious and emotional about dealing with an inappropriate comment at work.

However, it is better to work through the sentiments about the problem before addressing the case to ensure that you approach the conclusion in the most effective way possible. It can involve moving out of a room or having some fresh air and thinking about the issue for a moment.

Before taking any measures, it is better to consider how much annoyance the inappropriate statement poses in the company to determine what action to take. While some offensive comments may need a simple personal discussion, others require severe disciplinary measures from management.

In addition, if a colleague jokingly offends you but you think they had no malicious intentions, consider asking them about the remark at that point or having a personal discussion to present why their language was inappropriate.

Furthermore, if you hear a co-worker making prejudiced comments and being deliberately abusive regularly, reporting them to management is vital in order to keep the workplace secure for everyone.

Think about your position in the company and your level of accountability for managing inappropriate comments. If you are a supervisor or team leader, you must set an example for others that model ethical business values and handle unacceptable conduct in your group.

On the other hand, if you have an entry-level position, you may want to seek the aid of a manager or human resources professional to approach a higher-level workforce about their inappropriate remarks.

If a person makes an inappropriate remark during a professional discussion, you can begin by diverting the topic. It lets you remain on task and allows you to approach the person later to have a genuine dialogue about the comment if appropriate and refocus this discussion. Address the person making inappropriate comments privately.

One of the options for addressing an inappropriate remark is to invite the person for a private discussion with you. While you can also address the comment instantly after making it, waiting for a personal interaction gives you time to think about what you want to say about this issue.

In addition, if you're comfortable speaking to them, you can utilize this discussion as a chance to enlighten them about appropriate workplace conduct and hopefully enhance your working association with the person in the future. Ask them if they have some time to discuss the issue privately, away from any distractions.

Mention the inappropriate comment and ask what the person meant when they expressed it. Asking about the other individual's intentions can assist in avoiding any misunderstandings and offer them the benefit of the doubt.

In addition, knowing their intentions and being empathetic that every person makes mistakes can help you come to a successful solution. You may be capable of assisting them in realizing that what they said was abusive and be more considerate in the future.

Describe why the comment is unacceptable and summarize how their remarks impacted you or others. Explaining how you responded to the statement and how it made you feel can present another viewpoint and assist them in thinking analytically about what is appropriate to communicate in the workplace.

Concentrating on how the remark impacts others or causes problems in the workplace can present direct evidence of why they need to adjust their behaviour and control similar comments in the future.

Define the measures you want them to take or potential solutions to fix the issue. It can vary from simply abstaining from making similar statements in the future to issuing an apology letter for the inappropriate comment.

More severe problems may need solutions like diversity and unconscious bias training for the workforce. It can assist in stating that you understand that everyone wants to cooperate successfully and has the same objective of building a secure and comfortable organization.

When discussing the inappropriate remark, speak about the comment itself instead of judging the individual who remarked. It lets you remain neutral and objective while consulting a severe issue, especially when handling a statement in a group setting.

For instance, a person may be more open-minded if you say, "that statement is a rude stereotype of females and not suitable for work" than if you state, "you're sexist." The initial sentence points out the issue with an expression, while someone may notice the second phrase as a personal attack.

Closely consider how a person reacts when you approach them about an unacceptable comment. However, if a co-worker continues to make lewd remarks, you need to escalate the issue to the upper management. Furthermore, you can report the incident to the EEOC (Equal Employment Opportunity Commission) if the upper management does not take any action.

In addition, it is important to record repeated incidents of improper remarks, especially if they add to workplace prejudice or a hostile organization. Try interacting with the individual first but be proactive about taking a stand for yourself and others to foster a healthy workplace.

In a nutshell, employees must identify when offensive comments constitute workplace harassment to better report the incidents. In addition, the organization administration should remain equally considerate and make a safe work environment for their workforce.

Printed in Great Britain
by Amazon